# Skip's Pet Peeve . . .

Jason Dunnbar grinned at Skip. "Shouldn't you be home training your dog?" he asked. "So she doesn't totally embarrass you during Pet Week? Remember the time she ate those goldfish that belonged to a first grader?"

Skip glared at Jason. "She was practically a puppy when that happened. Besides, maybe I'm not going to bring Lupe to Pet Day," he said.

"Giving up?" asked Jason. "I don't blame you."

"No, I'm not giving up!" Skip snapped. "I'm just thinking of bringing a different pet, that's all. Something truly amazing. Something no one has ever seen before."

Jason laughed. "What're you going to do? Dye your dog's fur purple?"

"No," Skip said. "As a matter of fact, I'm not bringing Lupe. I'm bringing a different dog. A *very*, very different dog! In fact, I'm bringing a *werewolf*."

Other Skylark Books you won't want to miss!

# GRAVEYARD SCHOOL

## Little Pet Werewolf

# Tom B. Stone

A SKYLARK BOOK

Toronto  New York  London  Sydney  Auckland

RL 3.6, 008–012

LITTLE PET WEREWOLF
A Skylark Book / January 1995

ISBN 0-553-48226-2

*Published simultaneously in the United States and Canada*

PRINTED IN THE UNITED STATES OF AMERICA

OPM        0  9  8  7  6  5  4  3  2  1

# GRAVEYARD SCHOOL

## Little Pet Werewolf

# CHAPTER
## 1

**"Lupe, sit,"** Skip Wolfson commanded his dog.

Lupe just stared back at Skip. She yawned.

"C'mon, girl, you know how to sit," Skip insisted.

But then Lupe raised her back leg and scratched her ear—without sitting down.

Skip sighed.

Tyson Walker, who was hanging out with Skip in his front yard after school, shook his head. "Yeah, right, that's some cool dog you have there," he said sarcastically. "She's got a mind of her own."

"Well at least *I* have a dog," Skip said.

"*Low*," said Tyson. "I'll get a dog someday."

"When? When you get new parents?"

Skip, mostly without Tyson's help, was trying to train his dog, Lupe, to do tricks. He wanted her to win a prize during *Pet Week* at Grove Hill School.

But Lupe, a medium-sized dog with silvery fur who had been Skip's dog since she was a puppy, had other ideas.

1

She was always glad to go with Skip to the park or the playground, always glad to help him dig things up. She was very good at begging and sleeping and barking at imaginary dangers.

But she didn't like to do tricks. Skip had never been able to teach her a single one.

"Give it up," Tyson advised Skip. "Lupe doesn't get it. Never has, never will."

But Skip wasn't willing to give up so easily. "Lupe, shake," he said.

The big, shaggy dog opened her mouth and burped.

Tyson started to laugh uncontrollably. "Great trick! Maybe you could do a comedy act."

"Ha, ha," said Skip as he sat down on the steps next to Tyson. Lupe looked at them and wagged her tail, grinning a big dog grin. Watching his goofy dog, Skip couldn't help but smile back. He patted her head and scratched behind her ears as her big pink tongue flopped out of her mouth.

"What're you doing?" a voice behind Skip and Tyson whined.

Suddenly Lupe's ears pricked up. Her tail swished back and forth at hyper speed as she pawed the air in front of her and barked.

Skip groaned. His space had been invaded by his deeply weird little brother, Mark.

Lupe bounced up and practically danced up the stairs toward Mark. "Stay, Lupe," Skip ordered sharply.

"Well, what *are* you doing?" Mark whined again. He

stood at the back door with one hand in his pocket, his other hand raised, and his finger up his nose.

As usual.

"Don't do that!" Skip hollered.

"Do what?" asked Mark, taking his hand out of his pocket guiltily. He was clutching a dog biscuit.

Rolling his eyes, Skip said, "You know. Quit digging for boogers. At least in public."

"Oh." Mark took his finger out of his nose and wiped it on his pants. Lupe sat down at his feet and raised her paw again and whined.

"She wants you to give *her* the dog biscuit, freakface," Skip said. His little brother couldn't seem to do anything right.

"I'm not a freakface," Mark said, looking insulted. "And what if I don't want to give her the dog biscuit?"

Skip had just about had it with Mark. "Give Lupe the biscuit," he nearly growled. "It's mean to tease her."

"I'm not teasing her. She knows that." Mark stared down into Lupe's eyes. She was staring back intently.

Then, abruptly, Mark took a bite of the dog biscuit, turned, and ran back into the house. Lupe was after him in a flash. The screen door slammed behind them both.

"Lupe, wait! Lupe, come here!" Skip called. "We have tricks to do."

"She wants to go with *me*," Mark's voice answered triumphantly.

"Mark, come back here. Come back here now!"

No answer.

Skip gave up and sat back down. It wasn't worth the fight.

"What a psycho! I can't believe he actually *ate* a dog biscuit. Are you sure he's your brother?" Tyson asked.

Tyson was kidding, but Skip didn't answer the question right away. He was remembering when Mark was born.

Marcus Remulus Wolfson had had the biggest ears Skip had ever seen on a human being. And who ever heard of a baby born with a bunch of mouse-colored hair on his head? Not to mention his odd, enormous hands and feet?

"Your new baby brother," his mother had said, cradling Mark in her arms. "Isn't he adorable?"

"Uh, real cute, Mom," Skip had answered, "But, uh, doesn't he look kinda . . . you know, strange?"

His mother had looked hurt for a moment. Then her eyes had met his father's eyes. His father had cleared his throat and said, "He's a fine baby, Skip. You've got a big responsibility, young man. Being a big brother isn't all fun and games, you know."

Skip had given up. Clearly his parents were refusing to see that Mark didn't meet the standard for a normal-looking baby. Not like Skip. Skip often thought that he was the definition of normal—average height and weight, light brown hair, green eyes, with normal interests like movies and soccer. So how did Skip Wolfson, normal guy of the universe, end up with such a weird brother?

**4**

And it just didn't seem to get better when Mark got older.

Even though Mark had gotten over gnawing through the wooden bars on his crib—or anything wooden, for that matter—he still had many incredibly strange and annoying habits.

Like drooling uncontrollably.

Like whining and picking his nose.

Like stealing things and burying them in the backyard.

But did his parents see anything strange about Mark? No. Nothing Skip could say or do could make them admit that Mark had probably been dropped off by a space ship—rejected by aliens from a far-off planet.

"Dude?" said Tyson, waving his hand in front of Skip's face. "You still on the planet?"

Skip sighed. "Yeah," he said. "And no. No, I'm not sure Mark's my brother at all. In fact, sometimes I wonder if he's even human."

The monster turned. It growled. Red droplets glistened from huge teeth that shone in the light of the full moon.

"Shoot to kill!" screamed the blond man with the black eye patch. The men behind him all raised guns and began firing at the monster.

The monster frowned. Then it began to eat, one at a time, the men who were shooting at it. The monster used the men's guns as toothpicks to pull bloody chunks of flesh from between his teeth.

"Cooooool," said Mark. Lying on the floor in front of the television in the family room, he aimed the remote control and turned up the sound to hear the screams of the monster's dinner more clearly. "Listen, Lupe, isn't that great?"

The shaggy dog lying on the floor next to Mark thumped her tail on the floor. She didn't understand what Mark was saying, but the screeching cries from the television reminded her of the satisfying shrieks from the chipmunks she pounced on in the garden.

Mrs. Wolfson paused in the doorway to the rec room. "Aren't you boys supposed to be doing your homework?" she asked.

Mark smiled. The tip of his tongue stuck out just like Lupe's. "I've done all my homework," he said smugly.

"Skip?"

Skip glared at his little brother. "I'm working on it."

Mrs. Wolfson looked doubtful. But for once Mark helped Skip out. "Come watch, Mom. It's a super cool movie. The monster eats all the people trying to kill it and then it gets away."

"Well, it's a better deal than the dinosaurs got in *Jurassic Park*," Mrs. Wolfson joked as she glanced at the television.

"Yeah!" Mark agreed enthusiastically. He'd liked the dinosaurs in *Jurassic Park,* but that was about it.

Skip didn't want to admit it, but he agreed with his brother. It *was* sort of boring, watching the monsters always get it in the end.

"But haven't you seen this movie before?" Mrs. Wolfson asked.

"About a million times," Skip said. "He rents the same ones over and over at the vid store. And they're all monster movies."

Mrs. Wolfson smiled vaguely at them both. "As I remember, you used to be pretty fond of monster movies, too, Skip."

She started to leave and Skip thought he'd escaped. But she turned around. "Skip, finish your homework before you watch any more videos."

"Aw, Mom."

"Skip."

Skip raised his green eyes to his mother's golden brown ones. Behind the thick glasses his mother wore, her eyes were surprisingly piercing. Skip looked away quickly.

"Okay, *okay,*" he said. "Lupe, come."

Lupe didn't move.

"Lupe."

Lupe made herself flat against the rug.

"Fine. Stay," said Skip.

"Lupe likes me best. Ha, ha, ha," Mark said very softly as Skip left the room.

Skip heard him and whirled around. Mark quickly pointed the remote at the television and turned the volume up.

"Hey, freakface," said Skip.

Mark ignored him. Skip crossed the room and grabbed

**7**

Mark by the wrist. Mark yelped as Skip wrested the remote from his hand. He pointed it at the TV and muted the sound.

Skip glared at Mark as he gripped his brother's wrist tightly. Although Mark's eyes were the same golden brown as their mother's, they weren't quite as piercing. It was Mark who looked away this time.

"Don't push your luck, you little monster," Skip threatened. "You can watch all the monster movies you want where the monster wins, but let me tell you something. In real life the monster always gets it. Get it, *monster*?"

"Moommm," howled Mark, trying to pull free of Skip. "Moommmmmmm!"

Disgusted, Skip let go. "Lupe, come!" he ordered furiously.

Lupe raised her head and stared at him.

"Lupe," he said. "This is your last chance. I mean it." She put her head back down.

Skip gave up. He stalked to the door.

"Skip?" Mark asked. His voice was innocent but his expression was sly.

"What now?" Skip asked impatiently.

"Can I have Lupe for first-grade Pet Day at Graveyard School?"

That was the last straw. "NO!" shouted Skip as he stormed away. No way was his creepy little brother going to take over his potentially prize-winning dog!

# CHAPTER
# 2

**"Hello, boys** and girls."

Skip's eyes met Tyson's and both boys tried not to laugh. The smooth, sickeningly sweet voice of Hannibal Lucre, the assistant principal of Grove School, oozed out through the loudspeaker.

". . . Don't forget our very own Grove Hill Elementary School tradition coming up," Mr. Lucre said. "Pet Week. We'll have prizes, fun, games. Each day will be Pet Day for a different grade—except the fifth and sixth grade will have to share a day, of course. Anyway, where was I? Oh, yes, and different classes will take turns bringing in their pets. Please remember to, er, clean up after your pets. We don't want to make Pet Week extra work for our school caretaker, Mr. Bartholomew. . . ."

No one dared to laugh at that. The kids took that statement very seriously. No one wanted to be on the wrong side of Basement Bart, as Mr. Bartholomew was known. He was a silent man who had the habit of appearing unexpectedly and catching kids breaking the rules of Graveyard School. Big and scary, the worst thing about him was his strange and piercing eyes. No one wanted Basement Bart on their case.

"And boys and girls, have I got a surprise for you!" Hannibal Lucre rambled on.

Even though Skip closed his eyes in boredom, he could just imagine the short, round assistant principal rubbing his plump hands together as he talked.

Sitting in the front of the room, Stacey Carter, who ran her own pet-walking and pet-sitting business in Grove Hill, whispered a little too loudly, "Mr. Lucre's bringing himself as a pet!"

A ripple of laughter spread through the room until their teacher gave them all an evil look.

"The surprise is . . . a brand-new prize for Pet Week. It will be given for the pet voted Most Special and Unusual by the whole school on the last day of Pet Week. The prize is a gift certificate! To any store in Grove Hill! Supplied courtesy of the Grove Hill Merchants Association."

That got Skip's attention. He sat bolt upright.

Then Mr. Lucre added, in case they were enjoying the news too much, "And don't forget—at the end of Pet Week, you all have a report due on an animal-related topic. This will count toward your grade in science and in language arts."

Skip groaned. So did the rest of the class. But he couldn't get his mind off the prize. . . .

• • •

The soccer field was alive with activity after school. Skip and Tyson practiced passing the ball to each other.

"Pet Week," Tyson said scornfully for about the millionth time. "Can you believe it? And *Pet Day*. I mean, what do they think we are, first graders?"

"Some of us are," Skip pointed out.

"We outgrew show and tell long time ago," Tyson went on. "Man, I hate this."

"You don't *have* to do it." Skip juggled the soccer ball off his head, trying to keep it in the air. He suspected that part of the reason Tyson was complaining was that he didn't have a pet of his own.

"I still have to do the report, don't I? *You've* got it easy," Tyson said. "Your parents own a pet store. They aren't behind all this, are they?"

The ball bounced wildly off Skip's head. "No!" he said. He raced after the ball and slowly dribbled it away from the goal. He turned. "At least, I don't think so. And they don't run a pet store, Tyson. You know that. They run a pet *supply* store. There's a big difference."

"They have animals in the window," Tyson said.

"Those are rescued animals. Strays. Abandoned pets. They're trying to find good homes for them," Skip explained.

He pivoted, feinted to the left, then took a shot at goal. Tyson smothered it.

Skip made a face.

"You always kick to that side," Tyson said. "Always."

**11**

"But the goalies on other teams don't know that," answered Skip, out of breath. "And it's my best side for shots."

Soccer practice was almost over for the day. A few kids were still practicing drills, but most of the team had headed for the bleachers to take off their cleats and put on their regular shoes.

"Two more shots," said Skip. He set up two balls and fired them to the goal, one after the other.

Tyson caught them both. "Cobi Jones you're not," he said.

"Neither are you," retorted Skip.

"Yeah, but at least I look like him," Tyson said, pointing to the short haystack of dreadlocks at the crown of his head.

Skip rolled his eyes and began to dribble the ball toward the bleachers. Tyson caught up with him and they passed the ball back and forth until they reached their backpacks.

"You had some nice shots," Maria Medina told Skip as he sat down next to her to take off his cleats. Jason Dunbarr, who was sitting nearby, snorted, but he didn't say anything.

"You had better ones," Tyson answered before Skip could reply. "*You* scored."

"That's what I'm supposed to do," said Maria. "I'm a forward." She waved at Kirstin Bjorg, who was the sweeper on the team. Kirstin was as tall as Jason, and even more fearless.

12

"You bringing your new parrot to Pet Week this year?" asked Kirstin as she came up.

Maria nodded. "I'm trying to teach him a Graveyard School cheer. If I win, I'm gonna use the prize to buy a new pair of cleats. The good kind, like they wore in the World Cup games."

"Me too!" exclaimed Skip before he could stop himself.

"You too, what?" Jason asked. "No one is going to win that prize except for me. *Understand?*"

Jason stared hard at Skip. Jason was bigger and heavier than most of the kids at Graveyard School. It was no surprise that he was the class bully. But his bully act lost a lot of steam when Kirstin Bjorg beat him in the elections for class president.

Jason stood and puffed out his chest at Skip. "Don't you have a mutt whose best trick is staying awake?"

"Lupe's a great dog!" Skip countered.

Tyson cut in to defend his best friend. "So, Jason, what superbeast are *you* bringing to Pet Week? Not that I'm interested in all this kid stuff."

Refusing to let Tyson get to him, Jason kept his cocky stance. "I haven't decided yet. . . . But anything's got to be better than that furball of yours, Wolfson."

"Oh yeah? *Oh yeah?*" Skip sputtered.

"Isn't he the reason Mr. Lucre keeps reminding us to clean up after our pets? Or am I forgetting what happened last year?" Jason pressed.

"Hey, chill, all of you," Maria interrupted, before a

fight started. "Me and my parrot, we're going to win the grand prize. So you guys will just be fighting for second best." She and Kirstin gave each other a high five and walked away.

Skip was still fuming. "Maybe I won't bring Lupe this time. Maybe I'll bring another pet. I haven't decided yet."

But Jason wasn't fooled. "Yeah, Skip," he said. "You do that." He laughed and strutted away.

"Another pet?" said Tyson. "Your parents have told you no more dogs besides Lupe almost as many times as my parents have told me no dog at all. Where are you going to get another pet?"

Changing the subject, Skip said, "We better get out of here. It's getting dark."

For once Tyson didn't argue. He quickly finished unlacing his shoes and stripping out of his goalie gear.

Neither of them wanted to be caught around Graveyard School after dark. And although their coach would've given them a ride home, sticking around would have meant helping put the soccer equipment back in the storeroom. Neither one of them wanted to do that.

In spite of himself, Skip glanced across the field to the old graveyard that marched up the hill behind the school—the same graveyard that gave the school its nickname. No one ever was buried there anymore. And no one ever came to visit the graveyard.

At least, not by the light of day. And he wasn't waiting around to see who might hang out there at night.

Tyson finished packing his gear and the two of them

set off quickly for home, waving goodbye to their coach as they left.

It was Friday night and Tyson was staying over at Skip's house. As they walked, they made plans for an all-night pizza horrorthon.

"We could do some Frankenstein vids," said Tyson. "Those are pretty cool."

"I'm sick of Frankenstein," said Skip. "I could build a better monster with one hammer tied behind my back."

"Yeah, but not a live monster."

"I've got one of those already," Skip said.

Tyson laughed. He knew who Skip was talking about. "How's Boogerbreath doing?" he asked Skip.

Skip said, "He hasn't changed since yesterday. Listen, don't say anything about going to the vid store when we get home, okay? I don't want to have to take Mark with us. He'll make us pick out one of the same dumb movies he's been watching lately."

"Check," said Tyson.

But when they got home, Mark and the baby-sitter weren't there. They dumped their gear off and made it out of the house unquestioned.

Skip's spirits lifted. It was the weekend. He didn't have any homework, he was on the way to the video store, and they were going to have pizza for dinner. It was going to be a great weekend.

# CHAPTER
# 3

**"What're you watching?"**

"*Dead Werewolves.* Lose yourself, pizzabreath," Skip told his brother. He and Tyson were sitting in front of the television, eating.

"Same to you only more of it," Mark said, shoving his piece of pizza close to Skip's face.

As Skip pushed Mark away, Tyson smeared red pizza sauce around his mouth. "Mmm. Pizza blood. Look at me. I'm a werewolf."

"You are not," said Mark, lowering his head and staring at Tyson warily beneath his brows.

"You wouldn't like this movie, okay, Mark?" Skip said. "The werewolf is gonna get it good. I can tell—so get lost."

"Look! The werewolf just bit the scientist. He's turning into a werewolf!" Tyson frowned. "I thought it was vampires that had to bite you, you know, to turn you into a vampire."

On the television screen, the werewolf's mate found the body and began to howl mournfully. Then the werewolf's body began to turn back into its human form. The howls of the werewolf's mate turned to snarls of fear and disgust. She made a hideous face and turned and ran.

"Geez, that werewolf *really* bought it," said Skip. "That was great. Totally disgusting!"

A chilling, horrible moan filled the rec room.

Lupe jumped to her feet and faced the door, the hair on her neck rising.

With a quick look to make sure the sound wasn't coming from the television, Skip said, "Cut it out, Mark! If you can't act normal, leave!"

Mark staggered sideways, dropping his slice of pizza. He moaned again.

"Cut it *out*," Skip warned again. Then he noticed the piece of pizza on the floor. "You're not going to yak or anything, are you?"

At the word "yak," Tyson jumped up and turned on the light.

Mark clutched the doorframe. He didn't look very good. In fact, he looked dreadful. His mouth hung open. His eyes were wide and glassy. His face was pale. Sweat beaded on his forehead and his hair stuck out—even worse than usual.

"Hey, I think he really *is* sick," Tyson said to Skip.

"Well, he better not throw up in here," said Skip. "Mom! Daddddd!"

Licking his lips, Mark let his tongue hang out of his mouth. Skip could see half-eaten pepperoni.

"Gross," he said. "Mommmmmmmmm! Dad!"

"What is it?" Mr. Wolfson rushed into the hall, pushing his thick glasses up on his nose.

"Mark's about to projectile vomit all over us!" complained Skip. "He—"

A hair-raising scream filled the room, drowning out Skip.

Mark clutched his stomach with one hand and pointed at the television with the other.

Skip looked over his shoulder and saw on the screen a full moon rising, while the scientist clawed wildly at the hair sprouting on his face.

But it wasn't the scientist who was screaming. It was Mark.

With another horrifying shriek, Mark turned and tried to run out of the room. He bumped into his father and began to wave his arms wildly.

"Mark? Son?" cried Mr. Wolfson. He looked over at Skip and said, "Turn that off for a moment, will you, Skip?" Then he leaned down and put his arm around Mark's shoulders and peered into his son's face. Mr. Wolfson frowned and pushed his glasses up again.

Skip closed his eyes, half-expecting his disgusting little brother to choose that moment to throw up.

But Mark didn't. He just moaned again.

Mr. Wolfson looked up at Skip. "Could you go get your

mother? She's out in the backyard. And Tyson, could you go get a wet cloth or towel from the bathroom?''

Skip dropped the remote and shot out of the room. Tyson joined him. Neither of them wanted to be around when Mark threw up, but they didn't want to miss anything, either.

When Skip returned with his mom, Mark was in his room lying on the bed. Mr. Wolfson had put the cold cloth on Mark's head and turned out all the lights except the dinosaur nightlight by the bed.

"What's wrong?" asked Mrs. Wolfson, hurrying into the room.

"Did he throw up yet?" asked Skip. Tyson, who'd been standing in the hall by the door, shook his head regretfully.

"I don't think he's going to," Tyson said. "Maybe it wasn't the pizza."

"I bet it was," said Skip. "The little jerk had pepperoni, meatballs, *and* sausage on his pizza. What does he expect?" Skip made a sour face.

"That's enough, Skip," snapped his mother, bending over the bed.

"Fine," answered Skip. "C'mon, Tyson. Let's get out of here before we get covered with recycled pizza."

They were watching the end of *Dead Werewolves* when Mr. Wolfson came in.

"Did Mark say anything before he got sick?" he asked Skip and Tyson.

Tyson shook his head.

"Nope," answered Skip. "He just moaned a lot. And he dropped his pizza on the floor. I cleaned it up."

"Thank you," said Mr. Wolfson, his eyes straying to the screen. He winced.

"Are you going to call the doctor?" Tyson asked.

Mr. Wolfson said, "He seems better now. We're just going to keep an eye on him and then take him in tomorrow—unless it gets worse, of course. He's probably just coming down with something."

Mr. Wolfson pushed his glasses up on his nose and ran his hand through his short, mousey hair.

Seeing how concerned his father was about Mark, Skip suddenly wondered if he had been wrong about something.

Suddenly, looking at his father, Skip had the strangest feeling that it wasn't his little brother who was the alien.

*Maybe it's me!* he thought in a panic.

What was it about his father that was making Skip feel that way? Skip stared, trying to figure it out. . . .

Mr. Wolfson glanced toward the television again. "Horror movies?" he said, breaking the spell.

"*Dead Werewolves,*" Tyson explained enthusiastically. "It's a new one. It's about these guys who're killing off all the werewolves and then this mad scientist figures out how to bring them back to life."

Mr. Wolfson sighed. "Horror movies," he repeated. "I guess it's normal for you kids to like them."

"This one's super. Wanna watch the rest of it with us?

We're going to watch it again and fast forward to the good parts."

"Thanks, but no thanks," replied Mr. Wolfson. "Don't stay up too late, now, okay?"

"Night, Dad," Skip muttered, turning his attention back to the television.

"If you change your mind, we rented *Attack of the Claw People,* too," Tyson added.

Mr. Wolfson chuckled and shook his head as he left.

"Your parents are cool," said Tyson. "They let you stay up as late as you want."

Skip shrugged. His parents also made entirely too much fuss over his little brother. Not that he was jealous. But it was pretty sickening.

After the *Claw People,* they put *Dead Werewolves* on a third time and got into their sleeping bags so they could fall asleep with the movie on. It grew later and later still. Finally, Skip and Tyson fell asleep.

Outside, unnoticed, the full moon rose silently over Grove Hill.

# CHAPTER
# 4

**The wolf was** hungry. It hadn't eaten since the last full moon. Now it needed food—more than just the mice and rabbits and other small animals that it normally ate.

It needed something bigger. More satisfying.

A wolf-sized meal.

And then it saw the figure in the moonlit clearing ahead. The human figure.

The wolf stopped and snarled in disappointment.

It was hungry, but it wasn't that hungry. Real wolves didn't eat people.

Except in an emergency.

The wolf threw back its head and howled at the moon. As the wolf knew would happen, the human turned, eyes wide with terror.

Humans were afraid of wolves. It didn't make sense, but most things humans did, didn't make sense.

As the wolf expected, the human began to run.

Good. If it had to eat human, the wolf at least wanted

to work up an even more ferocious appetite before dinner.

The wolf howled again. Then, softly, quietly, its eyes glowing in the dark, it began to chase its prey.

A shadow fell across the silver moonlight.

The wolf skidded to a halt. . . .

Skip sat up with a muffled shriek.

Rubbing his eyes, he looked around the family room. He saw the full moon through the window and realized that the light of the moon must have awakened him. That must have been it. It was just a dream, he told himself. He wasn't a wolf. And he wasn't being hunted by a wolf.

Skip yawned. And stopped mid-yawn. Lupe, who'd been sleeping at Skip's feet, raised her head. She stared intently into the darkness across the room.

"Lupe?" he whispered softly. "What is it?"

She didn't move.

Then Skip saw it. A dark figure standing in the shadows by the door.

"Tyson?" whispered Skip.

But Tyson was sacked out in the sleeping bag next to him.

The figure crept slowly across the room toward him.

Skip opened his mouth to try to say something. To scream something.

But he was frozen. As frozen as Lupe.

Closer. Closer . . .

Skip jumped up. "You little creep!" he whispered.

Mark stopped at the edge of the moonlight that fell on

the family room floor. He didn't move. He didn't speak. His eyes were wide open, staring at Skip.

Lupe whined softly, anxiously.

"It's okay, girl," said Skip. He stepped closer to his little brother. "Mark?"

Mark didn't answer. He stared straight ahead, his eyes pools of darkness. Skip raised his hand and waved it in front of Mark's face.

Mark didn't even blink.

"Geez," breathed Skip. "Sleepwalking." His little brother was sleepwalking.

Remembering that he had heard not to wake up a sleepwalker, Skip reached out and caught the sleeve of Mark's pajama top. He gave it a slight tug. "Come on, Mark. Let's go back to bed."

To Skip's surprise, Mark turned obediently. He followed his brother out of the room and down the hall and back to his own bedroom. Lupe padded slowly behind them.

In his room, Mark climbed back into bed. He lay with his eyes open, staring up at the ceiling. It was then that Skip realized the curtains were open. He closed them so that the room was dark again except for the nightlight by Mark's bed.

Mark's eyes still stared up at the ceiling.

"Close your eyes, Mark. Go to sleep," Skip whispered.

Mark groaned softly, then closed his eyes. A minute later he was breathing deeply, as if he'd never been up at all.

Shaking his head, Skip tiptoed back down the hall. What had made his little brother sleepwalk all of a sudden? Had the pizza really made him sick? Weird as Mark was, he'd never done anything like that before. Usually, it just seemed he never fell asleep.

But he must have been asleep to sleepwalk. Had Mark been dreaming? What had he been dreaming about? Where had he been going?

*Maybe,* thought Skip, as he finally drifted off to sleep, *the little dweeb is even more twisted than I thought.*

Mark didn't remember sleepwalking the next morning. "Are you sure?" he asked his brother. "Why don't I remember?"

"Because you were asleep, dummy," said Skip wearily. "That's why it's called sleepwalking. Get it?"

Looking disappointed, Mark countered, "Are you sure I was sleepwalking? Maybe *you* were sleepwalking. Maybe you just dreamed it was me."

"Why didn't you wake me up so I could see?" Tyson asked Skip.

"*Because,*" retorted Skip, getting annoyed. His mom came into the kitchen and felt Mark's forehead.

"You seem okay now," she said with an uncertain grin. "But I want you to take it easy today."

"Are you going into the shop today?" Skip asked hopefully, ignoring his brother.

"Yeah, I've got to come visit. I want to talk pets," Tyson added. "I have this idea for my Pet Week report."

"What idea?" asked Skip, looking at Tyson in surprise.

"It just came to me," replied Tyson proudly. "A report on pet stores. I thought I could use your parents' store as a model pet store."

"We're a pet *supply* store, Tyson. We don't sell live animals," explained Mrs. Wolfson. "We don't approve of that business. Do you know that over fifteen million dogs and cats are put to death every year? No one wants them. No one will take care of them. There are enough pets that need good homes at your local humane shelter or the ASPCA. We can't support careless breeders who keep letting their animals have litters of cats and dogs that are doomed to death. Why—"

"Mom!" cried Skip. His mother was clearly on a roll. Skip knew everything she was going to say—he even agreed with her. But Tyson looked sort of stunned. "Tyson and I just want to visit and ask some questions, okay? We have Pet Week coming up at school and we'd like some pointers."

Actually, Skip was hoping he could persuade his parents to let him adopt, even if only temporarily, one of the abandoned dogs for which they were trying to find a home. There was bound to be a dog that could learn tricks more quickly than Lupe. Or at least that looked as cool as Stacey Carter's bull terrier, Morris.

Mrs. Wolfson stopped for breath, her cheeks red. She smiled. "Sorry, kiddo," she sighed. "Guess I was getting carried away. No, I'm not going to the shop today. I'm going to work here at home where I can keep an eye on

Mark. But I'm sure your father would love to see you and Tyson. And to help you in any way he can on your report."

"*Cool,*" said Tyson eagerly.

The Animals' House, the pet supply store owned by the Wolfsons, was in the middle of the town of Grove Hill. Skip and Tyson rode their bikes there. In fact, Grove Hill was small enough that practically every place in town could be reached by bicycle.

They parked their bikes and headed for the door of the shop. Tyson skidded to a stop out front. He pointed to the storefront. "I thought your parents didn't sell pets."

"*They don't!*" Skip told him for what seemed like the millionth time.

"What do you call that dog in the window? And those kittens over there?"

"They're from the Grove Hill Humane Shelter," Skip explained. "My parents are trying to help them find homes."

Inside The Animals' House, Mr. Wolfson sat behind the counter, drinking coffee and looking sleepy.

"Hey, Dad," said Skip.

"Don't shout," answered Mr. Wolfson.

"I'm not!" exclaimed Skip indignantly. "You aren't sick, are you? I mean, it's Mark who's been acting weird and sleepwalking and all."

"Sleepwalking?" Mr. Wolfson said. "Mark?" He

frowned, then forced himself to smile. "No, I just didn't sleep very well last night. What's up?"

"It's Pet Week again at Graveyard, er, Grove Hill School, Dad," Skip started. Then he sighed mournfully. "I guess I'll just take Lupe, like always."

His father looked at Skip. "Lupe's a good dog."

"Except she follows Mark around all the time now," said Skip. "Anyway, I was hoping—"

"Great dog," interrupted Tyson, pointing to the dog in the window. "What kind is he?"

"A German shepherd mix," Mr. Wolfson replied. "Why don't you boys take him for a walk. Give him some exercise."

"Wow, could we?" chimed Tyson.

"Tyson!" cried Skip. Tyson was ruining his alternate-pet plan. Besides, Skip didn't see what was so great about the dog in the window. With one ear up and the other ear down, the dog looked goofy. And even though it had German shepherd markings, it was small for a German shepherd.

"Go ahead," Mr. Wolfson, looking pleased, urged Tyson. "The leash is right by the door. He's very good on a leash. Somewhere, sometime in his life, he had a responsible and caring owner. . . ."

But Tyson wasn't even listening. He grabbed the leash and let the dog out of its kennel. "Come on, Skip. Let's go!"

# CHAPTER
# 5

**"What a *nice* doggie,"** said an ice-cold voice. "Is he yours, Tyson?" Skip jumped in surprise. He didn't know why he jumped. He didn't know why he gulped and glanced wildly around and acted guilty. Beside him, Tyson froze, also looking very guilty.

Somehow, Dr. Morthouse, the principal of Graveyard School, always brought out in them an unexpected feeling of panic. *That's what principals are good at,* Skip thought.

Tyson stammered, "Uh, n-no. No, he's not mine." The way he said it made it sound as if they'd stolen the dog.

Skip raised his eyes to meet Dr. Morthouse's. It was completely unnerving to run into her on the streets of Grove Hill. He was surprised she ever left the school. "We're, uh, walking him for somebody," Skip said quickly. *Great,* he thought. *I sound as guilty as Tyson does.*

Dr. Morthouse's smile widened and, as usual, a glint of silver flashed. Some kids insisted the silver was really a silver fang. But no one had ever been able to tell for sure because Dr. Morthouse's smile wasn't something that anyone liked to look at for very long. "How enterprising," she continued. "A dog-walking service."

"Uh," Skip began, then stopped. He glanced at Dr. Morthouse's smiling face and looked quickly away.

She kept smiling and kept talking. "Will you be bringing a pet for the sixth-grade Pet Day during Pet Week? The sixth graders are our shining examples for the rest of the school."

Skip gulped. "Uh, yes. Yes. Yes. A super dog. I mean, my dog is super. I'm bringing her."

"Ah," said Dr. Morthouse, her smile disappearing in a nastily unsettling way. "How nice."

She turned her attention to the window and Skip realized they were standing in front of an old shop with the word TAXIDERMY written in gold script on a sign above the door. The sign was blistered and peeling and faded. A film of dust coated the front door and the window of the dark shop.

"Dogs—the domestic descendants of the noble wolf," Dr. Morthouse went on. "Wolves, you know, have been called the children of the night." She pointed.

Then Skip realized what was looking back at them from the other side of the window—a huge gray animal with glassy, golden eyes.

A wolf. It had to be.

**3 2**

"Is that a . . . wolf?" Tyson asked.

"Yes, of course," answered Dr. Morthouse. "That's what taxidermists do, you know—stuff dead animals to make them look lifelike. In this case, the taxidermist didn't do the wolf justice."

For once, and in surprise, Skip found himself agreeing with the principal of Graveyard School—at least, if she meant what he thought she meant.

The wolf looked lopsided and moth-eaten. Tufts of its fur had moulted to the floor of the shop window. A yellowing, curling paper sign in front of the wolf proclaimed it to be THE LAST TIMBER WOLF IN THESE PARTS.

"Such a stupid, stupid thing to do, to shoot an animal and then stuff it," observed Dr. Morthouse. "Particularly a rare and beautiful animal such as the wolf."

"Yeah, er, yes," muttered Skip. "I guess."

"I'm glad to see you have such intelligent opinions," remarked Dr. Morthouse. She smiled again and Skip flinched. Beside him, the dog pulled on the leash that Tyson was holding.

Dr. Morthouse nodded impartially at all three of them. Then she turned and strode away down the street.

The dog pulled in the opposite direction, toward the pet supply store. "Yeah, I'd feel safer in a cage when she's around, too, boy," said Tyson. To Skip he said, "Whew. Mondo weirdo. Let's go back to the store—I want to ask your dad if he and your mom will help with my report."

"They'll help," said Skip.

"You don't mind, do you?" asked Tyson. "I mean, you weren't going to do the report on something like that, were you?"

"No," said Skip. "I haven't decided what I'm doing my report on but maybe I'll do it on wolves."

"Wolves? That'd be decent," Tyson said, as the dog pulled him down the sidewalk.

Skip turned for one last look over his shoulder at the wolf and stopped.

He stared, his eyes wide in disbelief.

The wolf in the window slowly turned its head to look back at Skip out through lifeless, glaring eyes.

# CHAPTER
# 6

**"No way!"** gasped Skip, backing up.

Skip let out a yelp and spun around.

Ahead, Tyson turned. "What is it?" he called. He started back toward Skip.

"The wolf . . . the wolf," stammered Skip as Tyson came back up to him. He pointed a shaky hand at the window. "It moved. Just now. It turned its head and . . ."

"Sure thing," said Tyson. "Good one, Skip."

"No, really!" protested Skip.

He turned wildly back around to look at the wolf.

It was standing in exactly the same position as when Dr. Morthouse had been looking at it, staring at the wall on one side of the window with its head slightly down, its ears up.

Skip took a deep breath. Had he imagined the whole thing? Maybe that dream last night was making him see things. Skip was suddenly glad that he hadn't told Tyson or anyone else about that dream.

He forced himself to grin. "I almost psyched you," he said to Tyson.

"Sure, dude," Tyson said warily. He nodded toward the restless dog. "He's getting antsy."

They turned and headed back for the store. As they rounded the corner, Skip looked back over his shoulder.

He didn't know what he expected to see. The wolf staring at him? Howling at the sky? Crashing through the window to come after him?

Whatever he expected, it didn't happen. The enormous, shaggy gray animal stood silent and dusty in the window. *It could never move,* Skip thought. It was so ancient that the slightest movement, the slightest touch, would probably crumble it into dust.

*What a dope I am,* thought Skip, turning quickly away. *It must have been that movie. Yeah, that was it.*

No more *Dead Werewolves.*


Racing Tyson home from Graveyard School on Monday, Skip saw a familiar object ahead.

A soccer ball.

And following the ball were three familiar people—Maria, Kirstin, and Jason.

Skip braked to a halt and Tyson almost ran over him. "What're you *doing?*" Tyson complained.

Ignoring Tyson, Skip stopped Maria, Kirstin, and Jason. "We don't have practice today, do we?"

Maria shook her head and ran her hand through her dark bangs so they stood straight up. "Nope. But Jason

**3 6**

had his soccer ball with him, so we're going to the park to play. Wanna come?"

"Sure," Skip replied instantly.

He and Tyson began walking their bikes alongside their three teammates.

Jason smirked at Skip. "Shouldn't you be at home training your dog?" he asked. "So she doesn't totally embarrass you during Pet Week? Remember the time she ate those goldfish that belonged to a first grader?"

Skip glared at Jason. "She was practically a puppy when that happened. Besides, maybe I'm not going to bring Lupe to Pet Day," he said.

"Giving up?" chided Jason. "I don't blame you."

Kirstin turned to Maria. "Why won't they admit that your parrot is going to win?" she asked. She took the ball from Jason, dropped it on the ground, and began to dribble it toward the entrance of the park. Maria jogged alongside her and they began to pass the ball back and forth.

"No, I'm not giving up!" Skip snapped. "I'm just thinking of bringing a different pet, that's all. Something truly amazing. Something no one has ever seen before."

Tyson gave Skip a look.

Jason laughed. "What're you going to do? Dye your dog's fur purple?"

"No," Skip said. "As a matter of fact, I'm not bringing Lupe. I'm bringing a different dog. A *very,* very different dog!"

Jason tried to keep a straight face. "Really? What kind?"

**3 7**

"Rare. Really, really rare."

"A basenji? A keeshond? A borzoi?"

Skip wasn't quite sure he even knew what kinds of dogs Jason was talking about. So he shook his head. "Those are ordinary," he scoffed. "I'm talking an *extreme* dog."

"Whoa, maybe you're gonna bring a wolf, is that it? A real live wolf?" Jason sneered.

"Even rarer," Skip snarled.

"Skip?" Tyson interjected, trying to stop Skip before he went too far. But it was useless.

As they reached Kirstin and Maria, who were standing by the park soccer fields, Skip announced, "I'm bringing a wolf to Pet Day all right. But not just any wolf. This wolf is a guaranteed winner of the prize—a super wolf. In fact, I'm bringing a *werewolf*."

Everyone stopped and looked at Skip in silence.

Then they burst out laughing.

"Right. You bring a werewolf, you get my vote," Jason said.

Maria broke in, "Where are you going to get a werewolf? There's no such thing as a werewolf."

Kirstin countered, "Anything can happen. Are we going to play soccer or what?"

Tyson didn't say anything. He didn't have to. The look he gave Skip said it all: *You've really lost it, Skip. This time, you've gone too far.*

• • •

*Why did I say such a dumb thing?* Skip thought later, on his way home. Everyone had teased him the whole time they played soccer. *Why do I always let Jason get to me? What am I going to do now?*

*But maybe I could just get a wolf,* he thought, remembering, with a shudder, the wolf in the taxidermist's window. *Capture a wolf and pretend it's a werewolf.*

Wearily Skip pulled his bike into the driveway and dropped it. He dragged himself up the back steps to the deck and rested his soccer-tired body against the railing.

*Finally, peace,* he thought. *No Jason. No school. No soccer. Just rest.*

But then he heard the snuffling and panting coming from under the deck.

Leave it to his little brother to ruin his moment of peace and quiet. Without even bothering to look down, Skip said, "Mark, what are you doing under the deck?"

The snuffling stopped abruptly.

"Mark," said Skip, making his voice threatening.

"Woof. Woof, woof, Grrrrrr."

"Very funny. And *very* convincing. Like I don't know it's you."

There was a scrabbling sound and a grunt, and Lupe suddenly emerged from under the stairs. She shot a glance over her shoulder. Lupe looked as if she had been pushed out of her hiding place.

She looked up at Skip and gave a slight, quick wag of

her tail, then turned and tried to crawl back under the deck.

"No," whispered a voice. "Stay."

Lupe whined and barked.

"You are so dumb," scolded Skip. "Come out from under the deck. If Mom and Dad catch you digging any more holes around the house, they're gonna destroy you."

Another low growl answered Skip. In disgust, Skip stood up. "Okay, fine," he snapped. "It's your funeral."

He stood up and went in the back of the house.

"Dinnertime in ten minutes," his mother announced as he let the kitchen door slam. "Put your bike away and go wash your hands."

"My hands are clean," said Skip automatically.

"And tell Mark, would you?" his mother asked.

"Sure," replied Skip. "Mark's under the deck with Lupe, pretending he's a dog. I'll—"

"Under the deck? Is he digging holes again?" Mrs. Wolfson turned and pushed past Skip out the back door.

The little creep was going to get it, Skip thought, and it would serve him right. He decided to go around through the front door to get his bicycle. He'd just opened the door when something went sailing through the air beside his head and hit the front door with a thud.

The newspaper. "Hey!" Skip called. "Good shot!" He waved at the paperboy, a kid with glasses and hair pulled into a neat little ponytail at the nape of his neck. Algie was the kid's name. He was new at Graveyard School this year.

Skip took his bike to the garage and then walked back around the front of the house to pick up the paper and take it inside. As he walked, he slid off the rubber band that held the paper in a tight roll. He was going to use the band to try to pull just the top part of his hair back into a ponytail, the way the captain of the United States World Cup soccer team had.

The paper fell open as he dropped it on the hall table with the mail.

And Skip's jaw dropped.

He blinked. He looked back down at the headline of the paper.

The headline was still there. It wasn't the biggest story on the front page, but it was definitely on the front page:

WOLF ATTACK?

Snatching up the paper, Skip read the article. A farmer had reported that something had gotten into his chickens the night before. At first he'd suspected a fox or a wild dog. But then he had found enormous footprints in the dirt around the chicken coop.

"Looked big enough to be a wolf," the farmer was quoted as saying.

The article concluded by reporting that the last known wolf, a timber wolf, had been shot and killed just outside Grove Hill more than forty years ago.

"Skip! Mark! Dinner," shouted his mom. "Fried chicken! Come and get it!"

Skip looked back down at the article. *A wolf in the chicken coop,* he thought dazedly.

*Too many horror movies,* he told himself.

Then he remembered how the wolf in the window had turned its head to look at him.

He'd imagined it, of course. Too many horror movies.

But suddenly Skip felt relieved.

Wolves were everywhere.

They were taking over his life.

Maybe it wouldn't be so hard to get one for Pet Day.

# CHAPTER
# 7

**The yellow eyes** haunted him. Every time he closed his eyes that night, he saw them, intense and spooky.

Dead.

Dead.

Dead and stuffed, Skip told himself. He fell asleep and then woke up again. He turned restlessly in bed.

He slid his foot down to rest it under Lupe where she usually slept at the end of the bed. But Lupe wasn't there.

Skip frowned. "Lupe," he called softly in the darkness. "Here, girl."

Nothing moved. He reached over and turned on his light. Lupe was nowhere in the room.

Skip's frown deepened. He'd gone to bed early. Closed his door.

Mark, the junior monster and dog thief, had probably sneaked in and lured Lupe away with treats.

That had to be it.

Skip pushed back the covers angrily and got out of bed. He was going to pulverize Mark. Turn him into monster slime. Chop him up and personally feed him, bit by bit, to Lupe.

He'd almost reached the door to Mark's room when a faint, unmistakable sound stopped him.

Skip froze.

*Why didn't Lupe bark?* he thought.

But she didn't. Wherever Lupe was, she didn't hear what Skip heard.

Someone was fumbling at the back door of the house. Skip looked over his shoulder. His parents' room was at the other end of the house. Could he get there in time?

He couldn't dial 911. One phone was in his parents' bedroom. The other was in the kitchen.

*I'll scream for help, that's what I'll do,* thought Skip. Instead, he found himself walking quickly and silently toward the kitchen. When he reached the doorway, he stopped and peered cautiously around the edge of it.

The kitchen was empty.

The sound was coming from outside the back door. He heard the sound of a metal trashcan lid.

Some animal was getting into the garbage. Skip groaned. He knew he'd be the one who had to clean it up.

He stomped across the kitchen and threw open the door. He leaped down the stairs to land by the garbage cans, waving his arms furiously. "Shoo! Beat it! Go aw— AARRRRRRGH!"

Huge, gold eyes looked up at him. A gray furry snout and sharply pointed ears swung in his direction.

Skip froze.

The wolf licked its lips with its long, red tongue. It cocked its head.

Skip leaped backward and landed squarely in one of the garbage cans. It fell over and the bag inside broke. Garbage came slopping out all over him.

"No! Yuck! Help! Ick!" howled Skip, fighting to get to his feet. Garbage flew everywhere. He slipped on something slimy and fell again.

The back door opened. "Skip? What's going on here?" His father's voice sounded from the top of the back steps above him.

Skip managed to get to his feet. "Wolf! Dad, it's a wolf! Don't let it get me!" He flung himself at his father and felt his father's hands on his shoulders.

"Take it easy, son. What're you doing out here rolling around in the garbage?"

Trying to regain his dignity, Skip stepped back. He looked around. The night was dark and quiet. There was no sign of a wolf.

He attempted to brush off some of the guck that was sticking to him, but it was useless. He was going to have to take a bath. In the middle of the night.

"It was a wolf," he exclaimed, looking up at his father. "A wolf was in the garbage. The wolf that everyone's talking about."

Without his glasses, Mr. Wolfson squinted back at Skip. "A wolf, you say? In our garbage? Skip, you must be imagining things."

"I know what I saw," Skip practically shouted.

"Probably a dog that some irresponsible person is letting wander around loose. Come back inside. . . ." Mr. Wolfson stepped quickly back as Skip obeyed. "And let's get you cleaned up."

Skip didn't bother to answer. He knew what he'd seen. He'd recognize those golden eyes, that furry profile, anywhere.

The Wolf of Grove Hill had been in their garbage cans.

His father leaned out for one last look around, then closed the door. "A wolf in the garbage cans . . ." He chuckled. "I could've sworn it was just my son."

Taking a shower in the middle of the night felt stupid. Skip hated it. While getting out of the shower, he was brooding about all the injustices he suffered when he heard it again.

The wolf was back!

Skip grabbed the towel and wrapped it around him. He raced down the hall and pounded on his parents' bedroom door, not caring if he woke up the whole house.

"Dad! Mom! The wolf is back. It's in the garbage cans! You'll see!"

No one answered.

"Wake up!" Skip screamed in frustration.

A hand came down on his arm.

Skip leaped into the air as a hand clamped over his mouth. "Shhh, Skipper, it's me," hissed a voice in his ear.

Skip pulled free of the hand over his mouth and whirled

**46**

around to face his father in the darkness. He opened his mouth to say, "What're you trying to do, scare me to death?"

His father held his finger to his lips and then pointed down the darkened hallway toward the kitchen.

Of course. His father had heard the noise this time, too.

"Want me to go call the police?" Skip breathed. "The fire department? The newspaper?"

His father shook his head. Moonlight glinted off his glasses. He had remembered his glasses this time.

"The humane shelter?" Skip begged desperately.

Again Mr. Wolfson said, "Shhh." He stepped around Skip and led the way into the kitchen.

*Wait'll I tell Tyson,* thought Skip. Even if Skip didn't show up with a werewolf for Pet Day, capturing the wolf would more than make up for it. He could almost see the headlines: LOCAL SOCCER PLAYER AND HIS FATHER CAP-TURE WOLF OF GROVE HILL.

Not to mention the extra credit he'd get for his report.

His father walked quickly and quietly across the kitchen and opened the door.

And then Skip saw who it was.

It wasn't the wolf.

"Geez," he said, not even bothering to keep his voice down. "I don't believe this. This is totally useless."

His mega-weird little brother was sleepwalking again. He was standing just outside the kitchen door at the top of the steps, staring out at the night.

And this time, Mark had Lupe with him.

"Come here, Lupe," said Skip. "You little creep," he said to Mark. "I bet you scared the wolf away."

"Shhh," Mr. Wolfson said, taking Mark by the shoulders and turning him gently around and guiding him into the house. "Let's get him back to bed."

"He's all yours," said Skip in disgust. "Lupe, come here."

Lupe ambled reluctantly across the floor. Skip turned and marched back down the hall, his dog trailing after him. She stood for a moment by Skip's bed, then jumped up and curled herself into a ball at the foot of it with a sigh. Skip didn't like the way she kept looking toward the door.

"Have you been taking weird lessons from Mark, or what?" said Skip.

Lupe cocked one ear in his direction but didn't stop staring at the closed door of Skip's room. At last she lowered her chin to her paws. But she kept on staring.

When Skip woke up the next morning, she was gone.

Even though it was early, he stormed down the hall to his brother's room. He pushed open the door without knocking.

No one was asleep in the bed. Skip was about to turn and leave when he heard a soft *swish-thump* sound. He stopped and looked around the room.

"Lupe?" he said. The sound grew stronger. It was coming from under the bed. Sleeping under beds, his father had explained when Lupe was just a puppy, was something dogs did naturally. It was like a wild dog sleeping in its den in a cave or a hollow log.

Skip bent to look under the bed. Sure enough, Lupe's golden-brown eyes peered back out at him. She flattened her ears and thumped her tail harder. Then she began to scramble out from under the bed toward Skip.

A voice grumbled sleepily.

Also from under the bed.

Skip suddenly bent back down. Then he got on his hands and knees to get a better look.

Sure enough, his little brother was sleeping under the bed, too.

"I think you should get the little creep a dog," Skip said to his father. His father, who was reading the Sunday newspaper and drinking coffee, made a vague sound that said, I'm listening to your voice but not to what you are saying.

Skip and his father were the only ones awake.

"Dad!" said Skip.

"Keep your voice down," his father warned from behind the paper. "Let your mother sleep."

"Dad," persisted Skip.

Mr. Wolfson lowered the newspaper. He looked sleepy and cranky. "What, Skip?"

He *sounded* sleepy and cranky.

"I think you should get jerk junior a dog," said Skip.

"If you're talking about your brother, don't you think that's a subject he should be addressing with me?"

"No," said Skip. "I mean, I am talking about my brother. But he's so busy stealing my dog that he doesn't have time to ask you for a dog of his own."

Mr. Wolfson sighed. "I'm sure Lupe is just being protective. It was very smart of her to go with Mark when he was sleepwalking last night."

Skip hadn't thought about that. "Maybe," he said, secretly proud of his dog, "but she was sleeping under his bed this morning. And Mark was under there with her."

In the act of opening the paper to a new section, Mr. Wolfson stopped. "Really?"

"He's getting stranger all the time, Dad, I'm telling you."

A little smile tugged at one corner of Skip's father's mouth. "Well, it's just a stage, Skip. You let me and your mother worry about that, okay?"

"Dad," continued Skip.

Mr. Wolfson looked back down at the paper.

"Dad, what about that wolf I saw?"

"Skip," his father said in a no-nonsense tone of voice. He frowned across the table at Skip.

"Okay, okay," muttered Skip hastily. "Maybe we can talk about it later."

But he knew they wouldn't. He would just capture the wolf himself.

That way he'd be a hero, his parents would be sorry they'd ever doubted him, he'd ace his report, *and* he'd win the prize for the best pet.

# CHAPTER
# 8

**"Hey, Skipman,"** said Tyson. He sat down in the seat next to Skip's just as the last bell rang.

Their teacher began to take the roll, and the loudspeaker started crackling and sputtering. It would do that for at least five minutes, while the teacher finished taking attendance. Then the assistant principal of Graveyard School, the oozy Hannibal Lucre, would begin making the announcements for the day.

"Hey, Tyson," Skip said, his voice covered by the din from the loudspeaker. "Guess what I saw last night. The wolf."

"What?" said Tyson, with doubt in his voice.

"The *wolf*. I saw it. Last night. It was in our garbage."

"Not a werewolf?" joked Tyson. "Just a plain old wolf?"

"I'm *serious*. It was huge. It had yellow eyes. I was standing this close to it."

Tyson shook his head. "And then it ate you, right? Get real, Wolfson."

The loudspeaker suddenly stopped its stream of noises.

Skip's voice rose in frustration. "I'm telling the truth!"

He caught the eye of the teacher, who looked up at Skip from the front of the classroom.

Skip straightened up and tried to look like a model student.

"You're serious? You're really, honestly telling me the whole truth and nothing but?" Tyson whispered.

"It's not a pysch-out, I promise. I saw that wolf," Skip insisted.

Tyson whistled softly. "Wow. . . ."

"And I had a great idea—"

"No," interrupted Tyson.

"You don't even know what it is," Skip said.

"No, whatever it is. See ya later," Tyson said quickly as the bell rang.

"What we're going to do, see, is go on a wolf hunt," Skip told Tyson later at practice. "If I capture the wolf of Grove Hill, I'll probably get such a big reward I can *buy* those cleats. Not to mention the Pet Week Grand Prize."

Tyson had been avoiding Skip all day, wary of his idea. But Skip was finally able to pin him down at the end of soccer practice. They talked as they ran cool-down laps around the field.

Maria Medina passed them, going what seemed to be about ninety miles an hour.

"Hey!" shouted Tyson, glad for the distraction. "You're making us look bad."

"I don't have to do anything to do that," Maria's voice trailed back to them.

Skip looked at Tyson. Tyson looked at Skip.

The two of them took off after her, catching up at the final turn. They raced to the finish.

"Whew," panted Maria, leaning over and putting her hands on her knees. When she'd caught her breath, she straightened up and asked, "You want a ride home? My father's coming to pick me up."

"I'm on my bike," said Tyson.

"Me too," added Skip.

"He's going to be a little late," Maria said. She sighed theatrically. "I guess I'll just wait. . . ."

"We could do some drills until he gets here," suggested Skip.

Tyson groaned. "Didn't we just do that?"

"If we just sit around, Coach'll put us to work helping with the equipment and stuff," Skip pointed out.

"Good point," said Maria. "Let's practice passing and taking shots."

"The other goal, then," said Tyson, pointing down the field at the goal at the far end. "It has more grass on it."

The three of them wandered down the field.

At the far end of the field the coach finished collecting

gear and started carrying it into the locker room. On the horizon, the sun set.

"It's getting dark," noticed Maria, looking around. She glanced over her shoulder toward the old graveyard that marched up the side of the hill. She narrowed her eyes.

"What're you looking at?" said Skip, spinning around.

"Relax. It's nothing. Just the moon starting to come up. But that graveyard gives me the creeps, you know?"

"It gives everybody the creeps," said Skip.

A car horn sounded from the parking lot.

"There he is!" Maria passed the ball to Skip and headed at a quick trot back down the playground toward the parking lot.

Skip dribbled toward the goal for one last play. He practiced every fake and fancy move he could, but Tyson still nailed the shot.

"Good one," admitted Skip reluctantly.

Tyson grinned. "Yeah."

They turned and headed back across the shadowy field. The coach had just gone inside the locker room one last time. Maria's father turned the car out of the parking lot and headed back up the road toward Grove Hill.

"It's late," said Skip.

"Yeah," agreed Tyson. He began to jog. Skip joined him.

"How come we're always the last players to leave?" said Skip.

"Dedication," was Tyson's reply.

It was Skip's turn to grin. "About that wolf you're going to help me catch . . . ," he began.

But just then, a sound echoed over the playground. A sound so chilling, so piercing, so frightening that the grin froze on Skip's face.

The blood froze in his veins.

His feet froze on the track.

From high up above the graveyard, the sound rolled down through the graves and reached frighteningly toward them through the darkness.

It clutched Skip by the heart.

"Keep *moving*," Tyson said.

"It's—"

"I heard, I heard. Keep moving!" Picking up speed with every step, Tyson broke into a run.

"Hey," Skip shouted, "wait for me!"

The howl rose to the sky and fell back to earth.

They grabbed their gear without slowing down. They didn't even bother to take off their cleats.

"Should we tell Coach?" panted Skip as he and Tyson pedaled their bikes furiously out of the parking lot.

"Coach is inside. And I'm not waiting," said Tyson.

They hit the road at a top speed and tore away from Graveyard School.

But the sound followed them. Skip could hear it ringing in his ears. He could feel it crawling down his spine.

He'd never heard the sound before, but he knew what it was, just as Tyson did.

It was the howl of a wolf.

# CHAPTER

# 9

**They didn't slow down** until they reached Main Street in downtown Grove Hill. They didn't stop until they reached The Animals' House.

Tyson dropped his bike by the back door of the shop and leaned against the wall, gasping for air. "Okay," he said between breaths. "Let's say I do believe you about the wolf. How do you plan on catching it?"

"Bait," said Skip. "We dig a big hole and we cover it up so it doesn't look like a hole and we put some bait in the middle and the wolf walks out and—*bam*. He's caught."

"Yeah," said Tyson weakly. He didn't sound convinced.

The back door opened. "I thought I heard something," Mr. Wolfson declared.

Tyson and Skip both began to talk at once.

"Calm down, Skipper, Tyson," said Mr. Wolfson.

"But we did! We heard it! Tyson heard it too. Now will

you believe me? It's the wolf of Grove Hill! It was stalking us out on the soccer field!''

"It's true!'' gasped Tyson. "Definitely.''

Mr. Wolfson motioned for the boys to come inside. He closed the back door behind them. "We'll put your bikes in the trunk and I'll give you both a ride home. Then you can *calmly* tell your story.''

In the car, Skip's father had them repeat their story. He listened without comment until they'd finished. Then he asked, "Did either of you see the wolf?''

"No,'' said Skip. "I saw it last night, though.''

"And we both heard it loud and clear,'' added Tyson.

"Have you ever heard a wolf howl?'' asked Mr. Wolfson.

"Sure,'' said Tyson.

"You have?'' Mr. Wolfson sounded surprised.

"All the time on TV,'' said Tyson.

"Oh. Well. Maybe it was a wolf. But more than likely, whatever's causing all this fuss is a feral dog—that's a pet dog that's been abandoned and gone wild. Or more sadly, it could possibly be one of those wolf-dog hybrids.'' Mr. Wolfson made a worried face. "You're doing your report on wolves, aren't you, Skip? You should include that in your report.''

"It was a *wolf*. We know what we heard, don't we, Skip? . . . Skip?'' Tyson implored.

"What?'' said Skip. He was suddenly silent, looking out the window.

"I know what you think you heard, but let's just keep a lid on this for a little while," Skip's father said.

"Okay," Skip agreed distractedly.

"What?" cried Tyson in disbelief. *"What?"*

Skip uttered, out of the side of his mouth so that only Tyson could hear, "Later."

They had just passed by the old taxidermist's shop. The window was dark. But Skip could feel the wolf on the other side of the glass. Feel it watching. Feel it waiting.

And suddenly he knew that the wolf in that window was no ordinary wolf.

He had to take another look at that wolf—as soon as possible.

The wolf was still there.

Skip closed his eyes and opened them again to make sure. Then he checked the name of the street and the windows of the two stores on either side of the taxidermist's shop.

As if he hadn't lived in Grove Hill all his life. As if he didn't know his way around the town in his sleep.

He pressed his face to the window and tried to peer behind the wolf into the gloom of the shop. But the dusty darkness revealed nothing.

Skip couldn't believe he was doing this. He'd thought about it all through dinner. He'd allowed his parents to believe that he was convinced by their explanation that what he'd heard was a wild dog.

Or even the wind.

*Ha!* thought Skip, remembering.

Meanwhile, he hadn't told Tyson where he was going. Not yet. The idea was too crazy.

*So I've seen the wolf,* thought Skip. *Now what?*

Without much hope, Skip went to the door of the shop. He pushed down the handle.

To his amazement, the door slowly swung open. It was creepy. Just like something in a horror movie.

He stepped to the threshold of the door. "Hello?" he called. "Is anybody home?"

That sounded stupid, so he added, "Or at work?"

His voice echoed hollowly. He cleared his throat. "Anybody stuffing any animals in there?"

Glancing quickly over his shoulder to make sure no one on the street was watching him, Skip stepped into the musty-smelling gloom of the old shop. He closed the door behind him and jumped at the sound of a rusty jingle. Then he realized that a string of bells had been tied to the inside handle of the door, just as in his parents' store, to let them know when people came in.

Reassured somehow, Skip paused for a moment and groped on the wall. But no light switch met his fingers.

Why hadn't he brought a flashlight? He waited and gradually his eyes grew accustomed to the dimness. As they did, the outline of a glass display case emerged along one wall. He shuffled carefully forward and sneezed in the dust raised by his feet.

Something brushed his head, and Skip jerked back

with a strangled shriek. Looking up, his hand held pro-
tectively over his head, he realized that a cord for an
overhead light swung above him.

He reached up and pulled gingerly on the cord. For a
moment, nothing happened. Then a dim lightbulb flickered on. It flickered off and then on again, as if it couldn't
make up its mind.

The flickering lightbulb made everything in the room
seem to move. But at least, Skip thought, it was better
than total darkness.

He walked forward. The display case was empty. A
long crack taped with peeling, yellowing tape ran along
the glass on top. On the wall behind the counter, empty
plaques hung.

Had animal heads and stuffed fish once hung there?
Skip wondered. He was glad they weren't there now.

He turned toward the window. When he got within
arm's length of the wolf, something made him stop.

"Here, boy," he said softly.

The wolf didn't move. A thick coat of dust matted its
gray fur. Dust lay in a carpet around the wolf's big feet.
Dust even filmed the yellow glass eyes, making them
duller and deader on close inspection.

"Yeah," sighed Skip, relieved. "Yep, you are one
*dead* wolf."

He backed away from the window and turned. A heavy
curtain drawn across an opening at the back of the tiny
shop caught his eye.

Cautiously, Skip made his way toward the curtain. He

pushed it aside and sneezed as dust puffed out all over him.

The faltering light was almost no help there. He could barely make out an old desk, the drawers missing, and a chair tilted to one side on three legs. A door with a heavy padlock loomed at the end of the room.

Other than that, it was empty.

No wolves there, dead or alive.

He reached out and grabbed the curtain to push it aside.

The light in the store flickered one last time and then went out, plunging Skip into darkness.

Then he heard the rusty jingle of bells as the door of the shop was suddenly pushed open.

# CHAPTER
# 10

**Skip stood rooted** in place. He was instantly and uncomfortably aware of how late it had gotten. And that he was where he wasn't supposed to be.

Suppose it was the police, he thought. Suppose they catch me and arrest me for breaking and entering. But I didn't break in, the door was open. . . .

Somehow, he didn't think that argument was going to work.

Footsteps sounded faintly in the room outside. They paused. Skip could almost feel whoever it was staring at the curtain he was standing behind.

After a long moment, the footsteps turned and padded softly toward the front of the store.

There was a muffled shuffling sound, and then the footsteps padded away again. The rusty bells jingled and the shop fell still.

Skip waited a long, long time behind the curtain. But nothing moved. At last he inched the curtain to one side.

The shop was completely dark. The only light was the faint light coming from the dusty window.

Skip looked around the shop again, then back at the window.

The empty window.

His hands grew sweaty with fear.

Before, the light that came dimly through the front window had outlined a silhouette—the moth-eaten silhouette of the stuffed wolf.

Now there was no silhouette.

Skip forced himself to walk ahead, forced himself to lean forward to look in the window.

No doubt about it. The wolf was gone.

The only thing left was a wide path dragged through the dust and next to it, the prints of enormous paws.

"Keep digging," Skip ordered.

"Do you know where we *are?*" snapped Tyson. "We are on a hill above a graveyard. At night."

"We've got to catch that wolf," replied Skip.

Tyson remarked, "If it's a ghost wolf, this isn't going to stop it."

"I don't know what it is, but *keep digging,*" Skip pleaded.

"I'm digging, okay? But I have to go home soon. I told my parents I'd be home late, but not this late."

"We're almost done for now," said Skip. "Here, I'll take a turn." He reached down and pulled Tyson up out of the narrow, deep hole they'd dug, and jumped in.

"It's creepy up here," Tyson observed.

Skip didn't answer. At last he said, "Okay, that should do it."

Tyson leaned over, holding the flashlight. He clicked it on. "That is deep," he said. "You know what it looks like, Skip? It looks like a grave."

"It's not a grave," argued Skip. He put his hands on the edge of the narrow hole and hoisted himself up. "One more night should do it," he said.

Tyson shook his head skeptically. "How do you know the wolf will come back here?"

"Wolves are territorial. This is part of its territory now or it wouldn't have been howling, right? So it'll be back."

"And we'll be ready," added Tyson.

"We will," said Skip evenly. "We will." Now, more than ever, he was determined to catch that wolf!

The hole was as deep as they could make it, so deep that finally they had to take turns digging, one leaning over to help pull the other up the steep sides. It really did look like a grave. Tyson and Skip covered it with branches and leaves until it just looked like a messy spot on the ground. They worked quickly, without talking. They tried to work so that one of them was always watching the other's back.

Then, using an old tennis racket he'd found in the garage, Skip lowered the bait—a pot roast he'd taken out of the freezer at home—onto the middle of the trap.

"It's frozen!" Tyson objected.

"It'll thaw out," Skip promised.

"Won't your mother miss it?" Tyson asked.

"I'm sure my parents don't know *what's* in their freezer," Skip assured him.

Tyson looked over his shoulder. "Let's get out of here," he said.

"Okay by me." Skip had come to the unpleasant realization that although it took a full moon for wolves to enjoy howling, they were capable of wandering around the night at any time.

Even when the moon wasn't full.

"We'll check the trap every night after school," Skip explained. "If we catch the wolf, we don't want it to starve or anything."

"Right," chimed Tyson. "Come on, Skip."

Skip took one last look at the wolf trap with the pot roast sitting in the middle of it. He sure hoped it worked.

As the moon grew fuller, Skip felt himself growing more and more tense. He was having trouble sleeping. He was sure the ghost wolf was somewhere out there. He could feel it watching him. Waiting for him.

Then one night, just before the moon was full, Skip woke up for an unknown reason.

Skip was completely alone in his room, alone by the light of the silver moon. An involuntary shudder ran down Skip's back. He found himself getting out of bed to go stare out the window.

It was like the setting of a bad horror movie, except there were no clouds. The moon shone down steadily, serenely.

And from out of the shadows of the garage darted a small, familiar figure.

"Mark," Skip whispered. As he watched, Mark paused and looked back over his shoulder. Then, crouching low, he ran to the corner of the yard.

Once again, Skip found himself sneaking around the corner of the garage in the dead of night, holding a flashlight—and his breath.

Quietly, slowly, he tiptoed along the edge of the yard, keeping to the shadow of the hedge and bushes. He was glad the moon wasn't full, but it was bright enough to make him feel as if he were in a spotlight.

But nothing moved in the backyard.

Where had his little brother gone? What was he doing in the dark corner of the backyard—the wolf corner?

Holding the flashlight in front of him, ready to turn it on or throw it and turn and run, Skip crept closer and closer to the corner.

At last he reached the edge of it.

The corner was inky black. No matter how hard he stared, he couldn't penetrate the darkness.

Then he heard a faint rustling sound. And then a sound like Lupe whimpering.

"Mark?" Skip whispered in spite of himself.

The sound stopped.

Quickly, before he could think about it, he raised the flashlight and turned it on.

It shone on his little brother, in his slightly too large pj's, who crouched in the bushes in the corner of the yard.

Mark looked up, blinking in the bright light.

"Skip?" he said, with a confused expression on his face.

"Yeah. What're you doing here?"

Mark blinked.

"What're you up to?" demanded Skip.

Mark looked around. Then he said in a small voice, "I don't know."

"That innocent act works on Mom and Dad, but it doesn't on me," snapped Skip.

"It's true!" Mark crawled out from the bushes and stood up. "I must have been sleepwalking."

Skip studied his brother. Was he telling the truth? Or was he up to some other, weird kind of mischief?

"Come on, then. Go back to bed!" said Skip.

Obediently, Mark fell into step beside Skip. Skip noticed how frightened Mark was as he led him back into the house.

At his little brother's bedroom door he stopped. "Go back to sleep," he said.

Mark suddenly yawned, his tongue curling out. He stretched. "Okay."

Skip waited for a while longer in the hall, until he could

Mark was asleep, he turned and headed back out to the wolf corner.

Skip couldn't believe what he'd seen. He had to make sure, and he had to make sure now.

In the uncertain beam of the flashlight, he thought he'd seen a mound of dirt in the corner in the deepest shadows.

A mound of dirt that looked like a grave.

# CHAPTER

# 11

**It was a grave.**

It couldn't be anything else. A shovel was propped against the fence behind it.

Forgetting for a moment the darkness, the shadows, the lurking presence of the wolf, Skip squatted down by the mound of dirt.

Someone had put flowers on it. But no name. No dates.

"Geez," breathed Skip. He couldn't believe his eyes.

What was buried in their backyard? And who had put it there?

Skip rocked back on his heels and looked wildly around. The yard was empty and still.

Skip poked at the dirt. Just as he feared, the dirt was loose. If the dirt was loose, it would be easy to dig up.

And there was only one way to find out what was buried below. Standing up, he picked up the shovel.

Skip began to dig. He dug very, very carefully. He

didn't want to stick the shovel in and have blood come spurting out. Or brains. Or body parts.

After every scoop of earth, he flicked on the flashlight to make sure it was just soil he had on the shovel. Although the night was cool, he began to sweat.

A dog began barking in the distance again.

Skip kept digging. One shovel at a time. The grave grew deeper. The pile of dirt to one side grew taller.

More sweat poured off Skip's face, and his heartbeat sounded heavily in his ears.

As the grave got deeper, he shifted position so that no one could sneak up behind him and push him in.

Then his shovel struck something soft. Something that wasn't dirt.

"Arrrgh," gagged Skip. He jerked the shovel back. Holding the flashlight up, he turned it on and peered down into the pit of the grave.

An eye peered back at him.

He tried to move. He tried to scream.

He tried to think.

But all he could do was stare at the dead eye staring back at him.

Then he remembered, and remembering didn't help.

He knew where he'd seen that eye before.

It was the glass eye of the wolf from the taxidermist's shop. The long-dead timberwolf had been buried in a grave in Skip's backyard.

• • •

Skip didn't really remember shoveling the dirt back on the stuffed timberwolf's grave. He didn't really remember much of anything until he found himself standing in the doorway of his little brother's room.

His brother's nightlight was on. Its yellow glow was brighter than that of the moonlight.

It shone down over the empty bed.

Skip walked forward and peered under the bed. That was unoccupied, too.

Like a sleepwalker, Skip went back down the hall to his own room. Lupe was waiting for him, lying on the foot of his own bed. She lifted her head and watched him silently.

Skip sat down heavily on the bed by her. "You *know*," he began to say to her. His voice came out cracked and hoarse.

He cleared his throat. "My brother," he said again. "It's my brother, isn't it?"

Lupe didn't move.

And then Skip had his answer—the eerie, insistent howl of a wolf.

For the next few days, nothing made sense to Skip. He felt as if he was living in a nightmare. He stared at his little brother so often that Mark began to whine and complain.

After that he was more careful.

But the more he stared, the more he thought about it,

the more impossible it seemed. And the more he couldn't think of any other explanation.

Meanwhile, with each passing night the moon grew fuller. But the wolf trap stayed empty, the pot roast bait growing more and more gross as it rotted. Tyson argued for a new pot roast or some other kind of bait. "That smell will scare the wolf off," he protested. He wrinkled his nose. "Or kill it."

"It'll work," Skip said shortly. "After all, the wolf likes to go through garbage cans, doesn't he?"

Tyson shrugged.

Skip was losing sleep. A million times a night, it seemed, he got up and tiptoed down the hall to his little brother's room.

But Mark was always there, sleeping deeply, his curtains drawn tight. Usually Lupe was there with Mark, too. Silently she watched Skip come and go.

And then one night Skip sat up in bed, awakened abruptly from a deep sleep. Without thinking, he was getting up, pulling on his clothes, slipping down the hall to check Mark's room.

Again, Mark's bed was empty. Only Lupe remained, standing at the window, looking anxiously out through the open curtains, framed in the light of the moon.

Skip shut the door and hurried quickly and quietly out of the house. He went instinctively toward the garage and hauled out his bicycle. A minute later he was pedaling his bike as fast as he could through the dark, silent streets of Grove Hill.

Graveyard School loomed up out of the darkness like a giant tombstone. Skip forced himself not to look at it as he rode into the parking lot. He rode past it, head down, and pumped his bicycle up the road. The tombstones on either side of Dead Man's Curve passed in a blur. The bridge over the icy stream that cut through the graveyard echoed hollowly beneath him as he went over.

And up. And up. Up to the top of the hill. Up through the weeds and overgrown grass.

Up to the trap.

The moonlight shone bright on every detail of the hill.

The bait was gone. Something had crashed through the branches of the trap.

Skip pulled to a halt, his heart pounding. He'd gotten the wolf—or something worse.

He dropped his bike and walked slowly forward.

Nothing moved. No sounds came from the trap below.

Skip went closer. Closer. He stopped and looked around. He had the eeriest sensation of being watched.

At the very edge of the trap Skip stopped and dropped to his hands and knees. He leaned over. He peered down.

Golden eyes lunged straight up at him.

Skip screamed and jumped back.

But he wasn't quick enough.

Something caught the sleeve of his jacket, yanking him forward. For a moment, he clutched at the slippery sides of the trap with desperate fingers. Then he flew through the night, down, down, down into the dark pit with the wolf.

Skip landed hard. So hard it knocked the wind out of him. For a moment he lay still on the muddy bottom of the trap, trying to think. Trying to breathe.

Then he heard the snuffling breath in his ear.

He slowly turned his head. The wolf was staring at him, its face only inches away.

"No! Stay! Bad wolf! Good wolf!" Skip shouted. He rolled away. He slammed against the wall of the trap.

The wolf leaped toward him, eyes gleaming, mouth open.

Skip threw up his arms and prepared to die.

He felt the wolf's claws against his chest, his arms. He felt them on his shoulders.

Then the wolf was gone. It had used Skip as a ladder to get up and out of the trap.

Skip fell forward to his knees, gasping, trying to calm his racing heart.

Through his gasps, he heard it, above him—the thin, wavering, triumphant howl of a wolf.

Then he heard the wolf trotting away.

And Skip was alone in the trap.

The night grew colder. Skip tried digging handholds in the dirt so that he could climb out, but they crumbled away beneath his feet. He tried jumping. He tried calling for help.

But the wolf was gone. And no one else was around. At least no one alive.

Only the inhabitants of the graveyard just below.

It was creepy. So creepy that it wasn't just the cold that made Skip's teeth chatter.

But Tyson would come to get him, wouldn't he? Tyson would hear that Skip was missing and know where to find him. Wouldn't he?

Or maybe the wolf would come back and kill him.

"Help!" cried Skip feebly. "Help. Help!"

He went to one end of the trap and took a running start toward the other. The tips of his fingers just clutched the edge. He held on, clawing, fighting. But it was no use. One by one his fingers lost their grip.

He was about to fall back into the trap when a hand came out of the darkness and grabbed his wrist.

# CHAPTER
# 12

**For one awful moment** Skip was convinced that one of the skeletons had risen from a nearby grave. He jerked back and tried to pull free.

"No," he gasped.

Then a gruff voice, a human voice, commanded, "Come on."

Skip was jerked out of the trap in one swift, powerful motion and tossed on the ground like a fish. He lay there for a few seconds, and then saw who had saved him.

Mr. Bartholomew—Basement Bart. The caretaker of Graveyard School. A man everyone avoided and most feared.

Skip was no exception.

"AARRRRRRGH!" he screamed, jumping up so fast he surprised even himself.

"Hey, kid," said the gravelly voice. "What's goin' on here?"

"Nothing. Er, I was just leaving. . . ."

Skip began to back up with shaking knees.

Basement Bart extended a tattooed arm and grabbed Skip by his jacket.

"Ahhhhhhh!" shrieked Skip. He twisted loose and left Basement Bart standing there, holding his empty jacket.

"Hey, kid!" Basement Bart shouted. "Hey!"

Skip didn't answer. He ran for his life.

"Awesome," exclaimed Tyson when Skip told him the story the next day. "Hey, and you looked wiped."

"I am," confessed Skip. He didn't mention that by the time he'd made it home, he'd found his brother sleeping peacefully, with Lupe at his side.

He hadn't told Tyson everything that had happened.

"So do we re-bait the trap?" Tyson asked.

"Not yet," answered Skip. He shuddered. "I don't think the wolf is going to fall for it again."

"Well, you'll think of something," said Tyson. "You better, you know. Pet Week is next week."

"I know," said Skip. "I know." He didn't tell Tyson that he already had. He didn't tell Tyson that he'd decided to track the wolf down himself.

By midnight that night, the moon was riding high in the sky. And Skip was falling asleep wedged in the hall closet, peering out through the slightly open door at the door to his little brother's room. The sound of the bedroom door opening made him sit up, alert.

"Stay, girl," he heard his brother whisper to Lupe.

Through the crack he caught a glimpse of his brother's shadowy form passing by.

Quickly, Skip crawled out of the closet and set off in pursuit.

Mark didn't look back as he opened the kitchen door and slipped out into the night. He didn't seem to sense anyone behind him. But Skip was very, very careful not to make any noise as he followed his brother out of the house.

Pausing on the front lawn, Mark stared up at the sky. Then he abruptly bent forward and ran toward the shadow of the hedge along the street.

His heart pounding, Skip hurried after him. When he reached the hedge, however, he saw no sign of his brother. Then a movement at the far end of the hedge caught his eye.

Skip rushed toward it. He rounded the edge of the hedge just in time to hear the crash of a trashcan turning over. He skidded to a stop as a light came on in an upstairs window.

There it was—a wolf stood on its hind legs by a trashcan and peered down at the contents, a lid on the ground nearby. It had upright ears and golden eyes and soft grayish-brown fur. Its paws were enormous.

Skip blinked. It *was* a wolf. But it didn't look exactly like a wolf should look. . . .

A window opened. A woman leaned out. "Get away from that trashcan," she shouted. "Mangy dog!"

The wolf lifted its head and its long, red tongue lolled

out. It looked like it was laughing. The front door of the house opened and the wolf sprang away into the darkness.

"Hey!" shouted a man's voice. "Hey, you!"

Skip realized that he'd straightened up—and that the man was shouting at him. He took off, too.

A crescendo of barks led him to the wolf's path. Sure enough, he could see it up ahead, loping along the yards of the biggest, meanest dogs in the neighborhood. It seemed to be taunting them, playing with them, leaping lightly toward the fence, then spinning away.

The dogs were nearly hysterical and barked their warnings at the wolf.

The wolf loped on.

It wasn't easy keeping up. Skip wondered if that was how defenders in soccer games felt, running endlessly after the opposite team when it had the ball.

They reached the edge of town, and the wolf veered abruptly onto Grove Hill Road. The wolf stopped and raised its head, sniffing the air. Skip dropped to the ground, motionless.

The wolf swung its head left, then right, sniffing loudly. Then it turned and cut across a field.

"Geez," muttered Skip, still following the wolf.

At the far edge of the field the wolf stopped and stood up on its hind legs. The lone wolf surveyed the landscape on its hind legs like a person—it was a creepy sight.

Creepy. But it was just one more thing to confirm what Skip already knew.

The wolf dropped to all fours again and dashed forward, and Skip soon heard the wild cackling of chickens. A dog began barking, and a man's voice shouted from a nearby farmhouse.

All at once Skip saw chickens fluttering into the air, heard the farmhouse door open and slam with a screech of hinges, and saw the blur of a Shetland sheepdog racing out of the farmhouse. The farmer's outline loomed behind, his arms waving furiously in the air.

The wolf circled among the chickens once more and then lunged off.

Skip took off, too.

He was sweating and exhausted. How did the wolf do it? It didn't even seem to be tired.

When they had reached the road, the wolf turned back toward town. It settled into a quick trot along the roadside. When it reached the hill just outside town, it went out into the middle of the road. It sank on its haunches and began to howl at the moon.

The thin, wavering thread of sound pierced the night. The sound seemed almost joyous, obnoxious, pleased with itself. *Look at me,* it seemed to say. *Ha, ha, ha.*

"Little turkey," muttered Skip. But he was grateful for the chance to catch his breath while the wolf bragged, out in the middle of the road.

When it was done howling, the wolf got up and headed back through the outskirts of town. Reaching the hedge that edged the Wolfsons' yard, it stopped again. Its head swiveled toward the trashcan it had opened earlier.

The garbage can lid was back in place. The light on the side of the house had been left on, and Skip could see it clearly.

The wolf could see it, too. It tilted its head and rolled its tongue out in a cocky grin. It trotted forward, tipped the lid off the trashcan with a clatter, and poked its nose down.

Almost in the same moment something clacked, the wolf began to yelp, and the door to the house opened.

"Got you!" shouted the angry man's voice.

The wolf didn't wait around to argue. Tail between its legs, it fled, yelping loudly and shaking its head in an effort to get free of a large rattrap attached to its nose. It didn't even notice Skip as it raced around the corner of the hedge and dove into the Wolfsons' yard.

Caught by surprise, Skip stayed where he was.

A fat man in a short bathrobe came down the steps and bent over to pick up the lid. He peered down into the trashcan and chuckled. "Works every time," he said under his breath.

# CHAPTER
# 13

**Skip flopped down** on his bed, exhausted. His mind was racing.

He hadn't wanted to believe it, but he had to. He knew the truth about his little brother.

Mark was weird. No, Mark was more than weird.

His little brother was a werewolf.

*What do I do now?* wondered Skip. But before he could think of an answer, he fell asleep.

The next morning he woke up in his grubby, sweaty clothes from the night before. He was as stiff and sore as if he'd played a major soccer game.

But he didn't let that slow him down. He got up and got dressed in record time. He was sitting at the breakfast table with his mom and dad when his little brother walked into the room.

Mark's nose was red and purple.

Mrs. Wolfson gasped. "Mark! Sweetie, what happened to your nose?"

"My nose?" said Mark, with a totally unconvincing show of surprise.

"The one on your face," Skip couldn't help saying sarcastically.

Mark ignored his brother. He put his hand up gingerly and touched the tip of his nose.

"Son?" said Mr. Wolfson, emerging from behind his newspaper.

"I ran into the bathroom door last night," replied Mark.

"Nose first?" said Skip. "I don't think so."

"It's true!" whined Mark. "Unless maybe you punched me in my sleep!"

"Yeah, right, blame me," snapped Skip. "Why don't you just tell the truth?"

He watched in satisfaction as Mark's eyes widened.

Then Mrs. Wolfson said, "Quit picking on your brother, Skip. Mark, let's go put some first-aid cream on your nose."

"Aw, Mom," Mark complained, but he let her lead him back down the hall toward the medicine cabinet in the bathroom.

Mr. Wolfson watched them go, a frown on his face.

"You don't believe him, do you, Dad?" asked Skip. "I mean, that is so lame."

"Mmm," said Mr. Wolfson noncommittally.

"Dad?"

"I was like that when I was a kid," remarked Mr. Wolfson. He grinned ruefully. "Always crashing into things and falling out of things and tripping . . ."

Skip groaned and gave up. No way was he ever going to convince his parents that Mark wasn't just weird or clumsy.

No way was he ever going to convince them that Mark was a werewolf.

Even Tyson wasn't interested. Before Skip could get started, Tyson interrupted, "Guess what. It's a deal."

"What's a deal?"

"That I'll have the most decent pet on Pet Day. You are looking at the owner of a new dog."

"You got a puppy?" asked Skip, temporarily forgetting his own troubles.

"A dog. The dog at your folks' pet supply store. My dad's working on a fence around the backyard and I got to bring him home this Saturday. Just in time for Pet Day on Monday."

"Really?" Skip knew how much Tyson had wanted a dog—and how much his parents had resisted the idea. "How'd you change their minds?"

"It was the report that did it. I wrote about The Animals' House and pet stores and unwanted pets, see, and then I wrote about Patrick—that's what I'm calling my dog, Patrick—and it just broke 'em right down."

"Decent, Tyson. Truly decent," said Skip. Then he thought about his own report, the one about wolves.

The one that should have been about werewolves.

"Skip? You okay?"

"Yeah." Skip looked steadily at Tyson. "But I think I've figured out a way to catch the wolf. Will you help me? Tonight?"

"Believe it," vowed Tyson. His eyes shone with excitement.

"Meet me at midnight by my kitchen door," said Skip.

"I'll be there," Tyson said gravely.

The moon was as full and fat as it could be. And much too bright for Skip's taste.

He and Tyson crouched down beneath the bushes by the back steps.

"I heard something," whispered Tyson.

"Shh," said Skip.

The back door opened. Footsteps passed by on the walk.

Skip leaned out and watched as his brother stood in the middle of the front lawn, staring up at the moon. The pair watched as Mark instantly bent forward.

By the time Mark had reached the shadow of the hedge, he was running on all fours.

"Did you see anything?" asked Tyson, pushing forward to stare past Skip.

"C'mon," said Skip without answering.

When they reached the corner of the hedge, Skip tugged on Tyson's arm and pointed silently. He felt Tyson's arm jerk in surprise.

His little brother, Mark-the-werewolf, was running down the sidewalk ahead of them. As they watched, Mark made a wide circle around the house that had the rattrapped garbage can.

"It's the wolf," hissed Tyson. "How did you know he'd be there?"

"I'll explain later," whispered Skip. "Come on!"

They followed the wolf past the rows of barking dogs and watched it tip over a couple of trashcans.

Then they followed it out to the edge of town.

Was his brother dumb enough to go back to the same chicken farm again? Skip wondered. Or did he realize that this time, the farmer would be prepared?

To Skip's surprise, he was actually relieved when his werewolf brother cut across a different field toward a different farm.

As they approached the farm, they heard the soft, anxious bleating of sheep. Skip picked up his pace.

The sheep began to bleat loudly. Skip caught a flash of fur as Mark went over the top of the fence and into the pen with the sheep.

The big, white, panicky blobs galloped around in every direction in the moonlight. In the midst of them all, causing trouble and having a great time, was the little wolf.

It was like watching a television replay in slow motion. A dog began to bark. A light came on in the farmhouse.

Suddenly, Skip heard a yelp. A moment later, the little wolf leaped back over the fence and shot past them, his ears folded back and his yellow eyes guilty and wild.

"What's going on?" said Tyson. "That farmer and his dog haven't even gotten out of the house yet."

"I don't know." Forgetting to be careful, Skip stood up and peered at the dark form fleeing across the field toward the woods.

"What're you doing?" cried Tyson, yanking on Skip's arm.

But it was too late. A light came on above the sheep pen.

"Hey! You! Lousy kid! Wait'll I . . ."

A huge dog launched itself across the yard.

Skip took off. Tyson took off. By unspoken agreement they split up.

The dog followed after Skip. Skip ran with all his might toward the woods. Maybe he could lose the dog in the woods. Maybe he could climb a tree.

He looked over his shoulder.

Maybe he was about to be eaten alive by a vicious dog.

Then there was a yelp.

Skip reached the edge of the woods and turned to look again.

The dog was running back toward the house at top speed. Out of the corner of his eye, he caught a glimpse of a familiar shadow.

The werewolf.

Without slowing down, Skip started after it as it melted into the far woods.

But when he reached the road, the wolf was gone.

Skip stopped and bent over, hands on his knees, trying to catch his breath. He looked up Grove Hill Road.

Empty.

He looked over his shoulder toward town. The road was a flat, dark, silver ribbon with nobody on it.

He was alone in the middle of the night with a werewolf.

A werewolf who knew he was there.

A werewolf maddened by moonlight. A beast. A wild animal.

Skip straightened up and tried to think calmly. *Don't be silly,* he told himself. *It's your brother. Your brother would never hurt you.*

But it wasn't really his brother, he reminded himself. Werewolves couldn't help themselves. They had to hunt through the moonlit nights.

They had to kill.

Suddenly Skip found himself wishing he'd been a little nicer to his brother just the same.

And that was when the wolves began to howl all around him.

# CHAPTER
# 14

**Without thinking,** Skip leaped across the road and into the shadows of the trees and began to run.

He didn't think about where he was going. He didn't think about what he would do when he got there.

He just ran.

The howling stopped.

Were the werewolves stalking him through the woods? Running alongside him just out of sight?

The thought spurred Skip on until he burst out of the woods into a clearing at the top of a hill.

And realized he was on the hill above the graveyard overlooking Graveyard School.

*Oh, no!* thought Skip, skidding to a halt. Where was the wolf trap? What if he fell in again?

He turned to go back into the woods.

And an enormous wolf stepped out.

Skip stopped. He stepped back.

The wolf walked slowly forward.

Skip turned again. Even hiding in the graveyard was better than facing this enormous, silent beast.

Then a second wolf slipped up from between the graves. And with it crept a third wolf.

The little wolf.

"Aaaaah!" screamed Skip. "Get back. I've got a gun. With silver bullets."

The wolves formed a circle around him.

"I mean it. Stand back. I know who you are. You come any closer, you're all gonna be dead werewolves."

The biggest wolf took a step toward Skip. It stood up on its hind legs.

"AAAAAAAAAAAH!" Skip screamed and ran as fast as he'd ever run in his life. He didn't worry about the wolf trap. He didn't worry about ghosts.

He ran through the graveyard without slowing down. He shot past the school without even worrying if Basement Bart was lurking nearby.

He ran for his life, back along Grove Hill Road. Even when he looked over his shoulder and realized that the werewolves weren't following him, he kept running. His sneakers pounded loudly on the pavement. His heart pounded even more loudly against his chest.

As he reached the edge of town, he heard the footsteps behind him.

"Noo," he gasped and kept on running.

Something touched his arm. "I'll die fighting!" he screamed and swung his fist with all his might. It connected with something solid. A familiar voice cried, "OWWWWW!"

Skip stopped. The dark world danced in front of him. He reached up and rubbed the stinging sweat from his eyes with his still-clenched fist.

Tyson was standing next to him, one hand pressed to his ribs.

"What're you trying to do," Tyson panted. "Kill me?"

"S–Sorry." Skip looked over his shoulder. "Did you—see anything?"

"Yeah—your back smoking down the road. What happened?"

What had happened?

What could he say?

*My brother, Mark, is hanging out with a bad crowd? He's joined a gang of werewolves?*

Would Tyson believe him? And what if he did? The werewolves hadn't seen Tyson. Maybe if Tyson didn't know about the werewolves he would be safe.

"I—think it's a wild dog," Skip said at last.

"Are you *serious*?"

Skip nodded. "Yeah."

"I don't believe it!"

"It's true. I just did my paper on wolves, remember? And this guy doesn't act like a wolf. Wolves mostly avoid people—this one's going through garbage cans and hanging out around farms. And it's little, too. Too small to be a wolf, really."

"Really? That's too bad. Bum deal, Skip," said Tyson. "So what do you do now, report it to animal control?"

"They probably already know. But maybe I'll call them tomorrow."

Tyson shook his head. "Wow. I was *sure* it was a wolf. A real, live wolf."

"Me too."

They stood for a moment longer; then Tyson said, "Well, I'm wiped. I'm turning in. See you tomorrow."

"Later," agreed Skip.


His knees still shaking, Skip walked slowly home. The neighborhood dogs threw themselves at the fences and barked at him. But they didn't bother him anymore.

How could a mere dog bother someone who'd been chased by a werewolf? No, three werewolves.

*What do I do now?* wondered Skip. He thought and thought, his footsteps getting slower and slower as he reached his house. But he couldn't see any way out of this mess.

He couldn't fight the werewolves himself—he didn't have a gun, and how could he afford the silver bullets?

Besides, he didn't want to be the one who had to deal with Mark.

Mark, he decided, was his parents' responsibility.

There was no other choice. He was going to have to tell his parents. And convince them, somehow, some way, to believe him.

Skip wearily walked up the back steps and pushed

open the kitchen door. He didn't bother to be quiet. He'd have to tell his parents right away. He had run out of time.

It was now or never.

He reached over and flicked on the kitchen light.

He leaped back. "Noooo! NOOOOOO!" he screamed in horror.

The werewolves were in the kitchen waiting for him.

# CHAPTER
# 15

**"Get away,** get away!" screamed Skip.

The biggest werewolf stood up.

"MOOOOMM! DADDDDD!" screamed Skip. He darted around the kitchen, trying to reach the hall door. "HEELP!"

The little werewolf stood up and blocked his way.

Skip scrambled back until he bumped into the refrigerator. "What've you done with Mom and Dad?" he asked. He turned and stared wildly at Mark. "This is all your fault, you little creep. Where're our parents? What have you and your, your werewolf pack done with them?"

"Relax, Skip. Take it easy, son," said the biggest werewolf.

"You can't fool me, you . . ." Skip's voice trailed off. His mouth dropped open.

"Skip, darling, you'd better sit down," suggested the

99

other big werewolf. "We're sorry to do this to you, but there wasn't really time to do it any other way."

Skip's mouth moved. He tried to say something, but the only sound he made was a feeble *Uh*.

"Ha," said the little werewolf. "Ha, ha, ha."

"That's enough out of you, young man," said the big werewolf. "Sit."

The little werewolf sat.

"Dad?" said Skip uneasily. *"Mom?"*

"That's right," said his father—the biggest of the werewolves.

"No!" said Skip. "Did Mark bite you and turn you into werewolves?"

"That's not really how it works, dear," said his mom. "Sit down."

"I'll stand, thanks," replied Skip.

His mother sighed. "I'm sorry it had to happen this way. You see, you're not a werewolf."

"No kidding," said Skip.

"The trait sometimes skips over a child," explained Skip's father. "When it skipped you, we thought it might have skipped Mark, too. That's why we raised both of you without telling you anything about it."

"What?" said Skip, with obvious shock in his voice.

"But it didn't skip Mark," his mother added. "Although we were only recently certain of that. You see, you had some of the traits of werewolves—you were restless even as a baby during the full moon, you got along well with dogs, you have very good hearing and a keen sense of smell—all characteristics of werewolf pups. But for you, that was it. You went through the transitional period, which happens between the ages of five and seven years, and nothing more happened. No sleepwalking. No particular reaction to seeing werewolves portrayed in movies and books."

"Not me!" said Mark proudly.

Mr. Wolfson gave his younger son a look and Mark got quiet.

"So Mark caught us by surprise, a bit. He went so quickly from sleepwalking to full-fledged wolfling. . . . At first we even thought there might be a real wolf hereabouts. But of course, it wasn't. It was Mark, being a bad werewolf."

Skip shook his head. "A bad werewolf, Mom? He's been terrorizing the countryside. Not to mention the fact that he stole that stuffed wolf and buried it in the backyard."

Mark's face became uncharacteristically sad.

"Poor wolf. It's understandable, in the circumstances, Mark," Mrs. Wolfson reasoned.

Mr. Wolfson said, "It's what any young werewolfling might be expected to do—go out late, tease dogs, chase chickens and sheep. Test their powers. Go a little wild."

"A little wild? *A little wild?* You call turning into a werewolf being a little wild?"

"Well, he'll be learning how to behave from now on," Mr. Wolfson said sternly. "Being a werewolf isn't easy. The privilege of being able to turn into a wolf and be faster and smarter and superior to the human species carries with it a big responsibility."

"Privilege? Responsibility? You're *werewolves*," said Skip.

Skip's mother looked annoyed. "Would you please quit saying 'werewolves' in that tone of voice? You're a member of this family, too, even if you didn't develop the appropriate werewolf characteristics."

"I'm *not* a werewolf."

"I'm sorry, son. We've tried to make it up to you," said Mr. Wolfson. "Of course, you'll still need to learn the Werewolf Code of Honor. It's still possible for you to have a werewolf family of your own someday." He looked over at Mrs. Wolfson. "If you find the right, er, girl."

"Forget it!" retorted Skip.

"You may change your mind. You're young yet," said Mr. Wolfson.

Mrs. Wolfson stood up. "It's late and it's a school night. You need a bath—in fact both of you do."

"Aw, Mom," whined Mark.

"First we need to change. We'll just step outside for a moment, that's the quickest way."

Still in a state of shock, Skip watched the three werewolves walk outside, standing upright. Then he staggered over to a chair at the kitchen table and slumped down.

He was still sitting there, staring at nothing, when his parents came back inside a minute later.

They looked so ordinary. His mom and dad in their

everyday jeans and big shirts and his scruffy little brother.

Or maybe not.

Nothing made sense anymore.

Mrs. Wolfson reached out and patted her oldest son on the shoulder. "It's okay, Skip. Just give it time."

"I guess." Skip looked from his mom to his dad. "You don't, er, kill people?"

Mr. Wolfson frowned intently. "People kill people," he said. "Animals mostly avoid them."

"What about all that stuff on the movies and in the books?"

"A bit of truth is contained in much of it," said Mrs. Wolfson. "But much of it is ignorant and exaggerated. Ignorance is another unfortunate human characteristic. But you'll learn more about it as you study the Code of Honor," she added. "Come on now. We all need to get a little sleep."

Skip stood up. "Okay," he said at last. It was going to take some getting used to, but he could see there might be advantages to the whole situation.

"Okay," he repeated. "I just have one favor to ask."

"Of course, dear," said his mother.

He looked over at his little brother. As a little brother, Mark was the pits. But as a werewolf . . .

Skip grinned at his wereparents. "May I take Mark to Pet Day?"

_Create your own kooky pet by solving the puzzle!_

First, write the answers next to each clue. Then copy the numbered letters into the same numbered empty spaces on the next page. When all the blanks are filled in, you'll have the name of a wild new pet! Have fun drawing the crazy creature, too!

## WHAT AM I?

1. I come from Australia, I'm tall, and I carry my babies in my pouch.

Answer: I am a

\_\_\_\_ \_\_\_\_ \_\_\_\_ \_\_\_\_ \_\_\_\_ \_\_\_\_ \_\_\_\_ \_\_\_\_.
                                  5       7

2. I have four legs, a long neck, and spots.

Answer: I am a

\_\_\_\_ \_\_\_\_ \_\_\_\_ \_\_\_\_ \_\_\_\_ \_\_\_\_ \_\_\_\_.
  8           2

3. I have wings and a beak, and my favorite meal is worms.

Answer: I am a \_\_\_\_\_ \_\_\_\_\_ \_\_\_\_\_ \_\_\_\_\_.
                              6

4. I'm plump; that's why people use me for my meat and my milk.

Answer: I am a \_\_\_\_\_ \_\_\_\_\_ \_\_\_\_\_.
                   1       3

5. I have wings and a beak, but I can't fly very far. People love my eggs, though.

Answer: I am a

\_\_\_\_\_ \_\_\_\_\_ \_\_\_\_\_ \_\_\_\_\_ \_\_\_\_\_ \_\_\_\_\_ \_\_\_\_\_.
                              4

Mystery pet:

\_\_\_\_\_ \_\_\_\_\_ \_\_\_\_\_ \_\_\_\_\_ \_\_\_\_\_ \_\_\_\_\_ \_\_\_\_\_ \_\_\_\_\_
   1       2       3       4       5       6       7       8

(Turn page to draw your crazy new pet.)

Draw your new pet here: